Ba

Barcelona

PHILIP LANGESKOV

DAUNT BOOKS

FOR ANNA

First published in 2013 by
Daunt Books
83 Marylebone High Street
London W1U 4QW

1

A CIP catalogue record for this title is available
from the British Library.

ISBN 978 1 907970 48 1

Typeset by Antony Gray
Printed and bound by
TJ International, Padstow, Cornwall

www.dauntbooks.co.uk

FOR THEIR TENTH wedding anniversary Daniel had arranged for them to spend a weekend in Barcelona, hoping to surprise Isla both with the fact that he had remembered at all and with a reminder of their honeymoon, which had also been spent in Barcelona. The idea struck him a few weeks before the actual date and it immediately felt like an important thing to do. In order to arrange accommodation at such short notice – it was the weekend of a crucial Barça *v.* Real derby game and the hotels were full – it had been necessary to contact an old friend of Isla's, Josep, who lived in the city, and who Daniel had met once or twice in London, and who had, on those one or two occasions, said that if they ever wanted to visit they should let him know and they could stay in his apartment, which was near the centre, while he would vacate and stay with friends for the duration of their trip. Daniel would rather not have done this – Josep and Isla had had a fling once, years ago, when they were students, long before he and Isla had met – but he could think of no alternative if the trip was to come off as he had imagined it.

Planning everything out in his head brought Daniel a great deal of satisfaction. He could not wait to see Isla's reaction, both to the whole event and to the little things he had lined up for when they were there: small things mostly, like coming upon a certain view at a certain time of day, or appearing to end up by accident at a bar they had got drunk in on their last visit. It would be such a surprise for her, all of it. And such a boost for them, as a couple. They hadn't done anything like this for years. Of course, Daniel swore Josep to secrecy and had no reason to suspect anything until, when he told Isla, one evening after work, the two of them drinking in the kitchen, that he had booked a trip for the coming weekend, the weekend of their wedding anniversary, she reacted not with shock or delight, but with calm assurance.

'Oh darling,' she said. 'I can't.'

'What do you mean?'

'I mean I can't. I have something on. I'm sorry. You should have said.'

'What do you have on? There's nothing on the

calendar.' As he said this, Daniel gestured to the back of the kitchen door. He was sure he had checked, sure he had looked closely; he remembered doing it, as if it were yesterday.

'Yes there is,' she said. 'Look.'

Sure enough, when he looked again, there was something – the scrawl of Isla's tiny handwriting – in one of the little boxes. He had to peer closely to make out the words: *Conference (Warwick)*.

'When did you put this in?' he said.

'Weeks ago,' she said. 'I'm sure I mentioned it.'

'Weeks ago? But I checked.'

'You can't have done, honey,' she said.

Daniel didn't quite know what to make of it, this apparent blindness on his part, and could only blurt out: 'But it's our wedding anniversary.'

'I know. I know. And it's important.' Isla spoke slowly, in what Daniel recognised as her serious voice. She really wanted him to know that this was as important to her as it was to him. She ran her hand along his sleeve. 'Love,' she said.

He didn't respond.

'Love,' she said again, looking directly into his eyes. 'We could do something another time, couldn't we?'

Daniel was conscious that he was on the verge of sulking. It was a struggle to decide whether it could be justified or not, whether a case could be made. The importance of the weekend, the value that he had attached to it in his mind, swirled around him. From his perspective, he knew, its significance had become outlandishly inflated. It was, after all, only a couple of days, but to Daniel those days had come to seem possessed of a precipitous, life-altering power. And all that thinking he had done, all that imagining: places to go, restaurants, moments to remember. It was, now he came to think of it, a reaffirmation of his commitment to Isla and he wanted it to be recognised as such. He hadn't even considered that it might go wrong, or, if he had, he had done so in a minor key: a bad meal in a supposedly good restaurant, being ripped off by a taxi driver, losing something. In the end, he decided not to speak. He just folded his arms and looked at his feet.

'Love,' Isla said again. She had moved round to stand in front of him. 'We can talk about it later, but I have to get ready. I'm meeting Grace, remember?'

This might be the limit, he thought, not for the fact, but for the timing, the moment when sulking becomes inevitable. 'Where are you going?'

'Just for a drink.'

'But.' He was about to gesture once more

towards the calendar, then realised that it would be ridiculous. He knew everything about this drink with Grace. Isla had told him, had invited him, even implored him to come. 'We'll talk about it later?' He hadn't intended to make it sound like a question, but that's how it came out.

'I'm sorry,' she said, taking her glass upstairs. 'We will talk about it later. Promise.'

After Isla had gone out, Daniel spent the evening mooching round the flat. He couldn't settle on a single spot. He lay on the couch, on the bed, he sprawled in the armchair in the study. As he did so, he mused over everything that had transpired. Josep must have told her, he thought. The dirty bastard. He had half a mind to ring him up and ask him, but decided against it. What did it matter, really? Josep was Isla's friend, not his; there should be no surprise as to where his loyalty might lie. At the kitchen table, on his laptop, Daniel looked into the possibility of changing flights. There was a fee, but it could, as far as he understood the website, be accomplished. Fine, he thought. They could simply go another time. It wasn't a big deal, nothing to get upset about. He opened a bottle of beer and congratulated himself on his equanimity. In fact, the more he thought about it the more he became convinced that another weekend would be better. They could stay in a proper hotel, for one thing.

When Isla returned, however, she was in a different mood. Daniel was already in bed, reading. When he heard the door go, he pretended to be asleep. He listened to the sound of Isla dropping her bag in the hall, easing off her shoes. When she entered the bedroom, she sat alongside him and began to stroke his hair. He could smell the wine on her breath.

'You're awake aren't you?' she said.

Daniel smiled, but kept his eyes closed.

'I'm sorry about earlier,' she said. 'It was just a surprise. I didn't react very well.'

'It's all right,' he said, opening his eyes. 'I should have asked. We can change the dates. I've looked into it.'

'No. You were right. We should go at the weekend. It's our wedding anniversary.' She smiled.

'Are you sure?' Daniel wondered what role Grace might have played in getting Isla to change her mind, what level of sacrifice this whole new mood implied. 'I mean, we could go another time. I really don't mind.'

'I'm quite sure,' she said.

'What about Warwick, the conference?'

'Balls to Warwick. You're my husband. It's not

as if I'm giving a paper or anything.' Then she added, as what seemed an afterthought, but which could just as well have been a theatrical diversion to conceal the fact that she already knew the answer to her question: 'Where are we going?'

'Don't you know?' he said. 'I thought you knew.'

'What do you mean? Of course I don't know. How would I know?'

'Just wondered if a little bird had told you.'

'No. No little bird. Where are we going?'

'You'll see.'

'This is intriguing. Which little bird? Do you mean Grace? Does Grace know?'

Suddenly Daniel felt much better, as if a weight had been lifted. Perhaps Josep was reliable after all.

On the Friday, as they were leaving the apartment for the airport, Daniel grabbed, at the very last moment, on a whim, the copy of Graham Greene's collected stories from the table in the hall. A colleague, Steve, had lent it to him months ago, after Daniel and Isla had watched *The Third Man* and liked it. Daniel hadn't got round to looking at it and thought that maybe the flight would be an opportunity. Then he could give the book back to Steve, lifting another weight from his conscience.

Isla was in a chirpy mood as the taxi weaved through the streets around Paddington Station. She kept looking at Daniel, touching his arm, and asking: 'Where are we going?' To which he replied with a smile and by raising a finger to his lips: 'It's a secret.' Of course, at the airport, he would have to reveal their destination, but he maintained the suspense for as long as he could, watching her as she tried to work it out, the expression on her face changing. When it finally dawned on her, as they neared the departure gate, she broke into a grin.

'Barcelona!' she said.

Daniel opened the book on the plane, shortly after they had levelled out. Isla was already asleep next to him, which he didn't think anything of at the time. He browsed the contents page, looking for the shortest story he could find. He wanted a quick fix, a hit, something that he could get into and out of in the least time possible; something that he could race through and get to the end.

The shortest story was called 'The Overnight Bag'. It concerns a man, Henry Cooper, travelling by plane from Nice to London, carrying an overnight bag. At the information desk he is given a telegram. It is from his mother. She wishes him a safe journey and looks forward to seeing him on his return. So far, so normal. As he read the story, Daniel felt a pleasant flash of recognition. On the one hand, this was because he knew the airport at Nice, could imagine its location, and, on the other, because he and Isla had just passed through an airport of their own and, although neither he nor Isla were carrying what could be called an overnight bag, they both had hand luggage and had, on boarding the plane, been faced with the dilemma of what to do with it, whether to place it on the seat, under the seat, or in the overhead locker.

In the case of the story, Henry Cooper is very particular about his overnight bag. He places it 'tenderly on the ledge of the information desk as though it contained something precious and fragile like an electric razor'. Later, on the plane, he sets it down on the empty seat next to him and secures it with a seatbelt. When a woman, sitting alongside the seat on which he placed the overnight bag, asks him why he is being so particular, he replies that he doesn't want it shaken about. When she places her own bag on top of his, he reacts testily: 'I don't want it squashed,' he says. 'It's a matter of respect.'

As Daniel read, Isla shifted in her sleep, so that her face was turned towards him, rather than towards the aisle. Her head was back, her straight brown hair half covering one of her eyes. She had a vague, almost apologetic smile on her face, as if, in a dream, she was having an experience that was both pleasant and troubling at the same time. Daniel looked at her for some moments thinking this, trying to penetrate her consciousness, to glean her thoughts, before brushing his fingers down her cheek and returning to his book.

The woman reacts angrily to Cooper's concern regarding the bag: 'What have you got in your precious bag?' she asks. To which Cooper evenly replies: 'A dead baby. I thought I had told you.' This, as Daniel could well understand, sends the woman into paroxysms of bewilderment. She splutters that he shouldn't be doing this, that the baby should be in a coffin and not an overnight bag, that there must be regulations for this kind of thing. Although Daniel smirked, picturing what he imagined was a rather pompous old woman, he was forced to consider what kind of regulations there might be for the event of transferring a dead baby from one country to another. He was sure there would be several forms to fill in. From this, he found himself contemplating a possible sequence of events that might lead to him, Daniel, having to conceal a dead baby in his own hand luggage.

Cooper explains to the woman that his wife

didn't trust a foreign coffin. 'Then it's *your* baby,' the woman says. 'My wife's baby,' Cooper corrects her. 'What's the difference?' 'There could well be a difference,' he says, sadly.

Daniel paused. He didn't quite know what to make of things. Cooper didn't seem a trustworthy character, not that Daniel thought that mattered particularly, but his language seemed at odds with the reality it claimed and the effect was distracting. Well. He would carry on, to see if things would work themselves out. There was a bottle of water in the seat pocket in front of him and Daniel took it out and drank from it, rolling the water around in his mouth as if to extract maximum benefit. He felt an itch in his side and, having scratched it, lifted his shirt to examine the surface of his skin. Nothing there but a small red mark, as if he had been bitten by a tick.

He read what remained of the story. There was a rather bizarre and comic episode with a taxi driver, who drives Cooper home. Although it is a cold day, Cooper asks the cabbie to turn off the heating, out of concern for the dead baby. 'Dead baby?' the cabbie says. 'He won't feel the heat then, will he?' Boom, boom. When Cooper reaches home, his mother is waiting for him. He places the overnight bag in the hall. She has laid out his slippers. They talk a little about his trip and he relates a peculiar tale about a severed human toe being found in a jar of marmalade. When his mother goes to put on the shepherd's pie, Cooper goes through to the hall. 'Time to unpack,' he thinks. He has a tidy mind, we are told. And there the story ends. There is no further mention of a wife, a baby, and the true contents of the bag are left unresolved at the end of the story.

Daniel sat there with the book in his lap staring at the half-page of white space at the end of the story, where someone, Steve perhaps, had written, in pencil: *yes, well?* Daniel knew how this mystery annotator felt, or, rather, he knew how he felt and assumed the annotator felt the same. He turned back a few pages and began to read again, in case he had missed something, some clue. As he did so, however, the pilot announced their descent into Barcelona. Daniel didn't like landing. In preparation, he slid the book into the seat pocket in front and turned to Isla. She was still sleeping and when he tried to rouse her she responded slowly.

'Is,' he said, shaking her. 'We're landing.'

She opened her eyes and looked at him, bewildered, as if she were returning from another realm of consciousness in which she had not been herself. 'Already?' She glanced quickly to either side, and then put her hand to her chest. 'My god, what a dream,' she said. 'It was like.' She paused. 'I don't know what it was like. Have you got any water?'

Daniel passed her the bottle and then sat back, watching, as she drank from it.

'Have I really slept through the whole flight?'

'Yup.'

'Completely ridiculous. I'm not even tired.'

Daniel reached for her hand and then closed his eyes. The plane shook as it passed through some turbulence. He thought about the story. It troubled him, made him uneasy. He couldn't have said precisely why it troubled him, even to himself, but already, as they made their descent into Barcelona, swinging wide over the city lit against the dusk, it preoccupied him to an unusual degree. He squeezed Isla's hand. She squeezed back.

Daniel was still thinking about the story as they went through passport control. The queue moved slowly. What was it that upset him so? The obvious thing to think would be that it was the suggestion of the dead baby, that this in some way hinted to an unspoken sense of loss within him regarding the decision he and Isla had made – long ago, before they were married – not to have children.

They just couldn't be arsed, or so they told themselves. They were either working too hard or having too much fun. Although subsequently they talked it over from time to time, wondering about the difference it might have made to their lives and whether they had changed their minds, Daniel was clear that they had never regretted it. Yes, they had friends whose children they liked, spent time with, but they never wanted the same for themselves, they never felt a lack. It wasn't that. It couldn't be that.

In the baggage hall there was a further wait. Isla was still drowsy from sleeping on the flight and she leaned against Daniel, one arm around his neck, as he stood there staring at the unmoving carousel, occasionally and distractedly kissing her hair.

The more he thought about it, the more Daniel began to think that the story was actually unpleasant, offensive even. Some coldness at its heart had made him shiver and he was not grateful for the effect. He wished he had never read the story, wished he had never picked the book up from the table in the hall, wished Steve had never loaned it to him.

There was quite a wait before the carousel got going and the people waiting – an assortment of families, couples, groups, people on their own, whispering into mobile phones – gave all the signs of growing impatient. As he waited, Daniel came to think that his problem with the story centred entirely on the character of Cooper. He didn't like him, it was simple: didn't like the way he behaved, the way he turned so felicitously from one situation to the next, switching personas, fazed, it seemed, by nothing. Of course, Daniel, in thinking, had realised that there was no baby in the story in the first place, nor was there a wife. This made it worse, Daniel thought, grasping for a rationale for his distaste. They were all constructs of Cooper's imagination; versions of his life that he chose to wear in public like clothes, sending out a false message. Really it was this that Daniel didn't like, this duplicity. He couldn't think why it bothered him particularly now, except to say that it was suddenly as if he had been introduced to a certain quality in himself that either he had not known about or had chosen to ignore or worked hard to suppress.

Around him, groups of people made comments about Catalan efficiency, looked at their watches, harrumphed. The delay frustrated Daniel too. It was, for the time being, as if they were in an in-between state, both there, in Barcelona, and not there, held back, in some way restrained, kept in England, or on the plane. As a consequence, with the story occupying a considerable part of his brain, Daniel didn't feel able to concentrate on his actual thoughts; nor could he commit himself fully to the act of imagining the anniversary weekend to come.

Finally, a half-hearted cheer went up. The luggage carousel had started to move.

With Isla cross-legged on the floor and Daniel standing with his arms folded, they waited as bag after bag passed before their eyes. Other passengers came forward to collect their belongings, hoisted them onto their shoulders or onto trolleys and headed out through the automatic doors to the arrivals hall. Beyond it, Daniel could glimpse the darkening Barcelona night, its palm trees and taxis. Only once in his life had he had the experience of his bags not coming out onto the carousel. It soon became apparent that he was about to have the experience for a second time and was as if he knew it before it had even happened.

Daniel looked at his watch. They would be late for Josep, for one thing. More than that, they would be late to bed, which would mean they wouldn't want to get up early, which, in the normal run of things would be fine, but as things stood, Daniel had plans for the morning, things he wanted them to do, not booked exactly, but certainly mapped out in his mind. They could be flexible, of course, but still. As the time passed and the number of people left waiting dwindled, Daniel began to develop a competitive streak, cultivating a sense of enmity towards the other people waiting, making judgements on their respective predicaments, weighing up whether they deserved the arrival of their bags more than he and Isla deserved the arrival of theirs.

'It's no good,' he whispered to Isla. 'Just you wait and see. They've lost it. They've lost the fucking bag.'

'Wankers,' Isla whispered back, each time someone else went to collect a bag.

In the end, it was just the two of them and a man of roughly Daniel's age, with close-cropped blond hair, a blue suit and an open-necked floral shirt. He had first noticed the man back in England, at the departure gate, in the queue, and now here he was again. The carousel squeaked emptily along. Rather than looking at the man, Daniel concentrated his attention on the mouth of the carousel, looking for every advantage, willing their bag to arrive, while at the same time knowing, deep down, that it would not. In the game of his imagination, the question of whose bag emerged next had become a matter of life and death.

Eventually, a bag did emerge. From a distance, it

looked like theirs, but just as Daniel was thinking this, the man moved forward, with a glance across at them, as if he were fully conversant with the rules of the game, understood the gravity of the situation.

'That's our bag,' Isla said, whispering into Daniel's neck.

'Are you sure?'

'Yes.'

'Wait a minute,' Daniel said, not quite loudly enough.

At the carousel, the man, having lifted the bag off, paused. He examined the bag closely. He opened one of the compartments and peered inside, rummaging around with his hand. Eventually, he looked up at Daniel, one arm still in the bag. 'Actually, this isn't mine,' he said. 'It must be yours. Sorry.'

'I wondered,' Daniel said.

'Same type of bag,' the man said, calmly, before handing it to Daniel. 'Same colour and everything.'

'Well,' Daniel said. Now he looked at the bag, just to be sure. It was theirs. 'Thank you,' Daniel said. 'It is ours. Perhaps someone has taken yours by mistake.' He had meant to say it generously, but in the circumstances he feared that it sounded sarcastic, a little bitter even.

When he returned to Isla she squeezed his arm.

'Well done, darling, saving our bag from the nasty man.'

'I'm sure it was a genuine mistake,' Daniel said.

'Nonsense. He would have nicked it if you hadn't said something.'

After they had cleared customs, they stood outside the terminal waiting for the bus. The air was hot, oppressive. Daniel riffled through his hand luggage.

'Shit,' he said.

'What is it?'

'I left that bloody book on the plane.'

'Oh, love,' Isla said. 'Do you want to go back?'

'No. It's not worth it. We're late enough as it is. Maybe I'll call tomorrow. Only it's Steve's.' He was about to say something else, something about the story, about how it was probably a good thing he had left the book on the plane, when it became apparent that Isla's attention had been caught by something over his shoulder.

'Look,' she said. 'It's that man. The one from the carousel.'

Daniel turned and looked. It was him. He strode out of the arrivals hall. It appeared his bag hadn't arrived, he wasn't carrying one at any rate. He walked straight across the pedestrian crossing, causing taxis to stop, and got into a car that was waiting for him at the side of the road. A woman was in the driver's seat but she didn't turn to look at him as he got in. As soon as his door closed, the car moved off, the man's gaze meeting Daniel's as they drove past.

'Was he English?' Isla said.

'I think so. He sounded it, didn't he?'

Suddenly, Isla doubled over and yelped in pain. 'What is it?'

She gathered herself quite quickly, standing up fully and taking a deep breath, in the way that somebody does when encountering a challenge. 'I don't know.' She put her hand against her stomach. 'This sudden pain.'

'Where?'

'Where I'm touching,' she said. 'Where do you think?'

'Sorry,' Daniel said. 'Do you mean here?' He moved his hand to cover the spot.

'Yes, there. I'm sure it's nothing.'

'It didn't seem like nothing,' he said, taking her head in his hands.

She nodded. 'It's nothing. I'm fine. Just a cramp, or something. It's passed.'

Daniel took her in his arms and held her close, kissing her head and smelling her hair.

*

24

When the bus arrived, they got on. Daniel looked out of the window as they moved through the outskirts of the city, past car dealerships, warehousing, industrial estates. In the story, Cooper never got the comeuppance he deserved. This was the thing, this was why he was annoyed. He invented this line about the baby, creating, in the minds of both the woman on the plane and the taxi driver, the experience of a trauma that in fact had not taken place. Cooper's just desserts, Daniel realised, would have been to find himself suffering precisely the traumatic experience he had called into being for others.

'What's on your mind?' It was Isla. She reached for his hand. 'Are you all right?'

'I'm fine,' he said. 'Just thinking about the story I read on the plane.'

Soon enough, they were at Plaça de Catalunya. It was alive with people. They decided to walk to Josep's apartment on Calle Valencia. They had a map and it didn't seem far. It was about 11 o'clock. They strolled arm in arm through the evening crowds and Daniel at last felt the pleasant lassitude of heat and travel. This was what he had wanted from the outset: to be walking these streets, at this hour, with Isla at his side. The feeling washed over him at first, but then went deeper, as they caught sight of familiar things, half-forgotten, but no less powerful for that. There were restaurants they had eaten in, shops they had shopped in, buildings they had wondered at.

'It's good to be back,' Isla said.

'It is.'

As they left Passeig de Gràcia, the crowds thinned and they entered that region of Barcelona in which they had spent so much time wandering on their last visit, their honeymoon, ten years previously. Here, again, they saw the elegant apartment buildings, with their wrought-iron balconies, the intricate designs in the plaster. They felt, or at least Daniel felt, an immediate familiarity in that atmosphere of dusty night, the warm air, the shuttered shops, the little cafés still open, their tables set out on the street.

'Do you remember all this?' Isla said.

He smiled.

'Why are you smiling?'

'Because I was remembering all this just as you asked me.'

She squeezed his shoulder and they walked on, under the shadows of trees cast by the streetlamps, past the all-night florist, a chemist.

'We were so convinced we would live here,' Isla

said. 'Do you remember? I was going to get a job at the university.'

'There's still time,' he said. 'We still could.'

Isla didn't say anything for a few paces and then squeezed his arm again. 'Yes,' she said. 'We still could. Anything's possible.'

As arranged, Josep was at his apartment to meet them. Daniel could hear his voice, crackly, through the intercom, as he buzzed them into the building. In the tiny elevator, so small that the two of them with their luggage could only just fit inside, Isla held her hand in front of her stomach and winced.

'Is it that thing again?'

'Yes. Just a little, you know.'

'I know. Are you sure you're all right?'

In the light of the elevator, her face was pale. He lifted her hair out of her eyes and felt her forehead.

'There's no fever.'

Josep met them at the door. Although Daniel had only met him on those one or two occasions in London he remembered him well, as if, although he hadn't been conscious of it, Josep had occupied a considerable part of his subconscious mind. He didn't appear to have changed. In fact, it was possible he was even wearing then the same suit he had been wearing on the previous occasions Daniel had met him, a narrow blue two-piece, elegantly cut, and a crisp white shirt. His dark hair was, as it had been, cropped close, revealing a little bit of thinning at the forehead.

Josep embraced them both, Isla first and Daniel second, and then returned his attention to Isla, holding her face, cupping it in his hands.

'Isla,' he said. 'You are here.' When he said her name, his accent had the curious effect of making Daniel think that he was talking to someone else, someone who was not his wife but someone else's, someone who he had not in fact met until that moment.

Suddenly, Isla buckled over in pain once again.

'Isla!' Josep said, stretching the second syllable. 'What is it?'

Isla flicked her eyes in Daniel's direction, before looking at Josep. 'It's nothing. Just a cramp.'

'Are you sure, darling?' Daniel said. He turned to Josep. 'There was another one, at the airport.'

'Then we should call a doctor,' he said. 'Of course.' He spoke English very quickly, the words running into each other.

'No,' Isla said. 'It's not that bad. I just need a painkiller.'

'Come on,' Josep said, 'follow me.' He ushered her through to the bedroom, turning to Daniel to say that he could drop the bags there, where they stood, before taking Isla into what Daniel presumed was a bathroom. Daniel stood there for a moment, before following them through to the bedroom, where he put the bags on the bed. He stood and listened at the door of the bathroom, but beyond a vague murmuring of a male voice and then a female voice, he could make out little above the sound of the extractor fan.

Daniel went through to the main body of the apartment. It was extensive, stretching across the whole top floor of the building, a large living area at the front, a pair of chaises longues to one side, set at an angle to each other, and bookcases lining every wall. There were two balconies, with their shutter doors folded back. Daniel went over and stepped onto the balcony to the left. Across from where he was standing, there was another apartment building, more or less the same, the same shuttered windows, the same wrought-iron balconies, the same intricate detailing in the fascia. Again, he thought of their first trip, of how they had then aspired to live in just such an apartment block. He lit a cigarette. Perhaps because of the heat, the night, the street sounds and the familiar smells, it was easy to remember the pleasure they had felt on their honeymoon, the lightness and the gladness in their hearts – a kind of bursting sensation that had threatened to leave both of them in hysterics for no reason other than their happiness.

Daniel was thinking about this when Josep came to join him on the balcony. 'I'm sure it is nothing serious, but I have called the doctor. Just to be safe. He lives quite close by. He will not be long.' As Daniel motioned to go back into the apartment, he held up his hand. 'No. Stay. Finish your cigarette. She is resting. I have given her an aspirin.'

'What do you think it is?'

Josep smiled. 'I don't know. I'm not a doctor.'

'But what do you think?'

'I think it is nothing serious. Something with her stomach perhaps. She will be better after rest. The doctor will know. Maybe she's pregnant.'

'I think that's unlikely,' Daniel said, smiling.

'Yes, of course. Would you like a drink?'

Josep returned with two tumblers of whisky. They stood on the balcony and drank.

'Ten years,' Josep said, raising his glass. 'Amazing.'

'Yes. It is.'

'You know, when I first met you, I didn't think you were good enough for her, for my Isla.'

'But now?'

'Now, I think you'll do.' Josep smiled. 'You care for her very well. She tells me things. And this trip. It is obvious.'

'I know how lucky I am,' Daniel said. 'Don't think I don't.'

Daniel turned away and leaned on the balcony edge, looking out at the apartment block opposite. Beneath them, despite the hour, traffic roared down the avenue. 'I love it here,' he said. 'These apartment buildings.'

'Yes. It's not the same in London I think. Here we can see right into people's lives.'

Of all the windows in the building across from them, only two were lit. It was, after all, a Friday night and Daniel supposed that most of the occupants were either out, having dinner or drinks, or away from the city for the weekend. One of these windows, in the top right-hand corner of the building, gave on to a room that appeared to be lined from floor to ceiling with books, more like a library than an apartment. There was a man, or what Daniel thought to be a man, sitting at a desk, with a brass lamp, writing, or reading, or in some other way engaged in an activity for which sitting at a desk was necessary. In the other, lower down, two floors below, partially obscured by the half-open shutter door, a man lay on a sofa in his underpants watching a football match on a large television fixed to the wall.

'You would like her, I think,' Josep said.

'Who?'

'The woman at the desk.'

'I thought it was a man.'

'No. Woman. She is a professor. German. Quite well known in Spain. She has led a glamorous life. Her husband is an antiquarian book dealer from Colombia. You can visit his shop. It is just around the corner. I know him a little.'

'And what about him?' Daniel said, referring to the man in his underpants. 'He is a man, isn't he?'

'Yes. He is.'

'What can you tell me about him?'

'Nothing. I don't think I've ever seen him before.'

Standing there together, sipping their drinks, smoking, Daniel allowed himself to become engrossed in watching the young man. Really, he did very little. He watched the game, occasionally scratched himself.

At that moment, a buzzer rang.

'That will be the doctor,' Josep said, looking over the balcony, directly below. 'Yes, it is him.'

Daniel looked over the balcony too. Beneath them, fifty or sixty or seventy feet down, there was a man in a black suit. He held in his hand a briefcase. At the kerb, a black car, quite large, old. A Jaguar, Daniel thought, or a Daimler. Josep shouted down and waved, before taking a last drag on his cigarette, flicking it over the balcony and turning back into the apartment.

They waited and listened as the lift hauled the doctor up to their level. He was a short man, glasses, beard, grey hair, which was slicked back over a well-tanned scalp. Daniel was introduced. The doctor and Josep spoke. Daniel thought that there were certain words that he recognised, like husband and London perhaps. The three of them went through to the bedroom. It was dark and Daniel stood leaning against the doorframe.

'How are you darling?' he said, as Isla raised her head.

'Okay, I think. I'm sure it's nothing serious. It's ridiculous all this fuss.'

Josep then spoke to the doctor in Spanish. The doctor lifted Isla's t-shirt and poked at her stomach, his small hands like paddles. Isla murmured when he reached a certain point. The doctor said something to Josep.

'Can you describe what it feels like, Isla?'

'Like a swelling, like there's a ball in there or something.'

The doctor looked up towards Josep and nodded, after which Josep turned to Daniel and said that they should leave them – the doctor and Isla – to it. The two of them then made their way back through to the living room.

'It is okay,' Josep said. 'He thinks it is nothing serious. An inflammation, perhaps, something like that.'

'Good.'

'Another drink?'

'Why not,' he said.

Josep settled himself on one of the chaises longues and invited Daniel to sit on the other. As if understanding Daniel's thoughts, he said: 'It won't be long.'

'It's all right,' he said. 'I'm just a little anxious.'

'Of course,' Josep said.

There was silence between them for a minute as they both sipped their drinks. Daniel cast his eyes around the apartment. He was about to say something about it – about how nice it was, or how he liked it – when Josep spoke first.

'What plans did you have for your trip?'

'Well. We'll have to see. It depends on Isla, but there were certain things I wanted us to do, repetitions of what we did on our honeymoon, or things we didn't have time for. There was a place we visited last time we were here – over by the harbour, in Barcelonetta, hidden away down a back street, but I can't remember the name. I think I could find it, if it's still open. I have it in mind for us just to stumble over it and it to be the same as last time.'

At that point, Josep looked up. 'Ah, the doctor.'

Daniel turned around and saw him standing on the threshold to the room. He stood with his feet together and his arms in front of him, the fingers of both hands meeting. Josep went over to him, but the old man beckoned him into the hall. Daniel strained to listen, but not only were they speaking a foreign language, they were also whispering.

'Well,' Josep said. 'He thinks it is possible it might be an ulcer, but it is not serious. Isla should have it checked out when she gets home, but for now the doctor has given her something to help her sleep. She should be fine in the morning with rest, although rich foods won't be a good idea if that's what you had in mind.'

The doctor gathered his things. Daniel rose, went over to him and thanked him in Spanish. The doctor nodded, curtly, first to Daniel and then to Josep, before leaving. Again they stood for a moment listening to the workings of the lift.

'Strange little man,' Daniel said.

'He is,' Josep said. 'But very good, reliable.'

Eventually, Josep started moving around the room, gathering various things, car keys, a wallet.

'I would stay and keep you company,' he said. But I have to go to my friend, to Katya's. I am late and she has work early in the morning. You understand what I mean.'

Daniel nodded.

'There is food in the fridge, if you are hungry, or' – he walked past Daniel and out on to the balcony and pointed back down Valencia towards the centre of town – 'there is a little place two blocks away, open late. It's quite good. Steak and such.'

'Thank you,' Daniel said.

'Here are the keys and here, I'll write down my number in case you should need to contact me.'

They shook hands near the door. 'She'll be fine tomorrow. Just you wait and see.'

Daniel thanked him and held the door open, casting light into the hallway, as Josep waited for the lift.

After Josep had gone, Daniel went through to the bedroom. Isla was already in bed, under a cotton sheet, curled, with her legs brought up to her chest. She looked up at him, the light from the hallway causing her to squint.

'I'm sorry,' she said.

'What for?'

'You know.'

'There's nothing to be sorry for.'

'I was sick.'

'You were sick?'

'In the bathroom. I was sick.'

'My poor baby,' he said and rubbed her back. 'And how do you feel now?'

'I really don't know. A bit zonked. I suppose I just need to give the pills time to work.'

In this position they remained, looking at one another in the half-light, not speaking.

'What will you do?' she said.

'I don't know. I might read. I might go out for a bite to eat.'

There was a pause. 'You don't mind?'

'Mind what?'

'You're not angry, I mean?'

'Angry? God no.'

'About this. About me being like this.'

'I mind that you are like this, because I don't want you to be ill, but I'm not angry. Not at all.'

'In the morning I'll be fine.'

'You will. Now put your head down and get some sleep. I'll keep watch.'

She put her head down on the pillow and he

kissed her. He went through to the bathroom, splashed some water on his face, then sat on the toilet seat. His own head was throbbing from the heat. In a cabinet under the sink, there were some pills, he took the last two and put the empty packet in the bin.

He went back through to the bedroom and knelt by the bed. He intended to speak to Isla, to tell her that he loved her and that he would be there, in the next room, if she needed him. His arm was on her shoulder, which was bare above the cotton sheet. Her eyes were closed and she didn't move.

'Are you awake?' he said.

She didn't respond.

Daniel stayed there for some minutes, looking at her face. In the end he didn't do anything. He didn't wake her or speak to her or anything. He just watched her sleep, the rise and fall of her body.

After a little while, he got up and left the room, taking the bag he had used as hand luggage with him. He remembered that he had left his book on the plane, then he remembered the story. He would have liked to read it again, if only to work out why it was stuck in his head. He thought about how ridiculous this was as he went to the fridge to see what food there was. There was some cured ham, some Manchego and some quince jelly. He put some of the ham and cheese on a plate along with a spoon of the jelly and carried it to the dining room table, where he sat with his back to the open doors of the balcony. Just as he was about to raise the first morsel of ham and cheese to his mouth, he caught sight of an open bottle of wine on the counter, next to the sink, and went back into the kitchen to fetch the wine and a glass, before returning to the table. He poured the wine. The food was good, just what he needed. After he had eaten, he carried the plate back through to the sink and rinsed it.

He was tired, but not sleepy. Not wishing to lie in bed, awake, with the danger that he might disturb Isla, he sat for a little while in the only armchair and drank the rest of the wine. He felt the oddness of unfamiliar territory – the late hour, Isla asleep and him awake. He couldn't bring himself to read any of the books that lined the shelves of the apartment, most of which were in Spanish in any case. He went back out to the balcony.

He wondered about Isla, about how she was. Wondered what the doctor meant by an ulcer. How serious it was. He had heard of ulcers bursting, but that wouldn't happen. It couldn't. He was fantasising. Worse than that, he was catastrophising.

From where he was standing, it was possible to look down, at an angle, on the hexagonal junction of Valencia and one of the cross streets. Periodically, a little clump of taxis streamed past, the odd car, a motorcycle swerving at pace down the road. A gaggle of people stood on the street, smoking, fanned out around the doorway to a bar. Not far from them, Daniel's attention was caught by an old woman and an old man walking up the cross street and round onto Valencia. They were beneath him, but on the opposite side of the road. The woman was bent nearly double and carrying plastic bags with what Daniel presumed to be food inside. Certainly, he thought he could see a baguette sticking up, perhaps the outline of a bottle of wine. The old man was pulling what appeared to be a trolley behind him. It was only by looking closely that Daniel could see that it was an oxygen tank; from there he was able to follow the tubes that led from the cylinder to the man's nose. Every few paces the couple stopped, the woman putting down her bags, the man, drawing level with her, putting out a shaking arm and grasping her by the hand. After a time, a young woman broke away from the group outside the bar and came over to the couple. Although Daniel was high up, he could hear the sound of her voice.

She took the bags from the old lady, who touched her arm. Then they walked across the road and disappeared from view.

As he looked at the empty space that they had left, Daniel felt like the world was a very remarkable place indeed. It wasn't specifically because of the good act he had just witnessed, although it certainly helped. Even the couple by themselves would have been enough: the great sense of life that they hauled in their wake seemed to verge on the miraculous. Was it easier, he wondered, in a city like Barcelona – in a country like Spain, for that matter – to romanticise the lives of the old? Their history seemed more transparent, its lines more clear: you were either on this side or you were on the other side. Did he even think like this at home, or was it only here, or abroad in general, that he came upon thoughts of such a character?

He went through into the bedroom and got undressed in the dark. After brushing his teeth, he got into bed. Isla turned towards him in her sleep and mumbled something that he couldn't make out. He put his arm around her and pulled her to him. Whether it was the sight of the old couple, or Barcelona itself, or what, Daniel renewed the vow that he would do whatever he could to protect her, even to the extent of sacrificing himself.

The reasons didn't matter, but such things were easy to forget, with all the ins and outs of normal life. They had a chance of being different, however. Nothing was yet set in stone. He lay there for a little while in the dark, feeling both optimistic for the future and completely terrified by it. Just as he was on the point of falling asleep, an image drifted into his mind: Cooper, in the near-silence of his room, unpacking the overnight bag, his mother in the kitchen, dealing with the shepherd's pie.

The following morning, Daniel woke to find the bed next to him empty. He could smell the familiar scent of Isla's shampoo. The bedroom door was open and through it he could see all the way to the front of the apartment. The shutters were open and the sun streamed in. He called Isla's name, but there was no reply. He got up and pulled on a pair of shorts and walked through. He could see her on the other side of the window, sitting on the balcony in the sun.

'Morning,' he said.

'Morning, darling. You slept well.'

He kissed her head. Her hair was wet. 'What time is it?'

'Almost ten.'

'Ten! How did that happen?'

'I didn't want to wake you, not after all the palaver last night.'

'How about you? How did you sleep?'

'Not so well. I've been up for hours, just sitting here. The sun's lovely,' she said, stretching her arms above her head.

'What do you think you can cope with today?'

'I'm not sure. Not too much, perhaps, but maybe we could go out and get breakfast somewhere. I'm starving. Did you have any ideas?'

'I did, but we don't have to do any of them.'

When Daniel had showered, they left the apartment and rode the elevator down to the lobby, before stepping out into the sunlight of a Barcelona Saturday. It was fiercely hot – hotter than he had expected; it was only May. As they walked, Daniel's anxieties of the night before seemed to slip away. Everything was going to be fine; nothing was going to happen. They wandered for quite a time, eyeing up possible places to stop, feeling the heat on their backs and the pleasant sensation of being far from home. When they found that they were nearing the Sagrada Familia, they turned back. In the end, having almost done a complete loop, they sat down at a table on the pavement, a place just a couple of blocks away from where they were staying. They garbled their order apologetically in half-Spanish, half-English, but the waitress was sympathetic and brought them coffees and a selection of pastries. There were a handful of people sitting at other tables, reading newspapers, consulting travel guides.

'How's the pastry?' Daniel said.

'Not sure yet. It's a bit sweet. There's apricot in it or something.'

'I hate that,' he said. His own pastry was very dry, more of a cake.

When they had finished, Daniel lit a cigarette and offered one to Isla.

'That's better,' she said, once it was alight, puffing the smoke out with real satisfaction.

'What shall we do tonight, do you think? It is our actual anniversary after all. Do you think you'll be up to something? A meal, maybe? We could go back to that restaurant from last time.'

'Let me see how this goes down,' Isla said.

At that moment, her phone went. She answered it. It was Josep. Once Daniel knew that, he allowed their conversation to fade into the background. He watched the traffic, the play of the light through the trees.

When Isla finished the call, she related its contents. Josep had suggested that he take Daniel for lunch, allowing Isla to rest a little more, giving her the opportunity to be fully restored for the rest of their weekend.

'Is that what you want?' Daniel asked.

'I wouldn't mind a little more rest,' she said. 'What about you? Would you mind?'

'If you'd like me to go, I'll go,' he said. 'I never say no to lunch.'

'No, you don't,' Isla said and smiled. 'And it will be okay with Josep? He won't get on your nerves.'

'Not at all. We had a nice chat last night.'

She phoned Josep back and it was all arranged. Daniel had another coffee, they both had another cigarette. It was pleasant out there on the street and he was able to bat away all negative thoughts.

When they were done, they strolled back to the apartment. For the next couple of hours, they lazed on the balcony. Isla read some essays she had to mark and Daniel attempted a crossword in a newspaper he found in the bottom of his bag. Not long before two, Josep texted. He was outside. Daniel kissed Isla and went down.

Josep was parked by the kerb, in a convertible BMW. He had sunglasses on, shorts, his legs enviably brown and hairy. Daniel jumped in and they roared off into the traffic.

'How is Isla?' he asked.

'All right, I think. It's good of you to take me for lunch.'

'It's nothing. There's a little place I think you'll like. It's not special. In any case, you must save your energy for tonight.' He turned and looked at Daniel, a smile on his lips and, Daniel imagined, in his eyes behind his sunglasses.

Daniel smiled back. 'Now, now.'

'You know what I mean,' he said. 'Tonight's the night, no?'

'You mean our actual anniversary?'

'Yes.'

'Yes it is,' Daniel said.

They drove down a wide avenue, a grand arch ahead of them, set back in a park that Daniel remembered visiting before. There had been buskers underneath and he and Isla had danced, a little drunkenly, and had their photograph taken by a procession of strangers. Josep had his eyes on the road. They were driving towards the sea and soon it came into view, glinting, the sails of boats peaking the horizon. Daniel thought of Isla back at the apartment, the cool tiles beneath her feet. He hoped she was reading, or sleeping, or doing whatever it was that made her comfortable.

'She'll be okay, won't she?' he said, leaning over

to make himself heard above the traffic. 'I don't have to worry.'

'She'll be fine,' Josep said. 'Relax. We're nearly there.' He swung the car to the left and they drove down a road lined with restaurants, their tables spilling out onto the wide pavement. The vista seemed familiar. Away to the right was a large, low, sandy-coloured building. Daniel had seen it before. It was the maritime museum. 'We're not going here,' Josep said, nodding to the restaurants over to the left. 'This is for the tourists.'

He turned the car left again and drove slowly down a side street, white and terracotta buildings on either side. It was less grand than the area in which Josep lived and the smaller balconies in this part of the city were draped in flags, pledging allegiance to a bewildering array of what Daniel presumed to be football clubs. Again, it all seemed familiar. Then, as Josep pulled into a space on the left, it became apparent why. It was the very place that he and Isla had been to on their honeymoon, the one he had been talking about the preceding night as he and Josep stood on the balcony.

'But this is the place I was talking about last night,' he said.

'Really?' Josep said. 'I had no idea. This is a place I always visit.'

'And you had no idea?'

'None.'

He had no way of telling if Josep was in earnest or not. Perhaps Daniel had told him, or Isla had, long ago, after their honeymoon, and subsequently forgotten. Whatever the reason, as he walked along the pavement, Daniel telephoned Isla. He wanted to tell her about the extraordinary coincidence. You won't believe this, he was going to say, but the phone rang and rang, the unfamiliar ring tone of a foreign exchange, then it went to voicemail. Assuming she was sleeping, Daniel left a message, telling her not only about the restaurant, but also that she needn't feel any pressure about going out that evening; he would, he told her, be more than happy just to stay in and curl up with a book.

The restaurant was much as Daniel remembered it, only busier. The previous time, with Isla, had been a weekday and they had had a pick of tables. With Josep, however, they had to share a table with an older couple, a man and a woman, their faces as if worn from exposure to the sun. It was clear that Josep was a familiar presence, as he nodded to the waiting staff – all men, wearing dirty white t-shirts and blue jeans. A counter separated the tables from the kitchen, which stretched to the back of the building, maybe five chefs working away on various types of grill or surface. The counter itself was covered in open dishes, already prepared and ready to be picked up by the waiters and carried to the tables.

'Everything is good,' Josep said, raising one of two cold beer bottles, which had appeared in front of them. Around him, the room was alive with voices.

'I know,' Daniel said. 'I've been here before.'

'Of course,' Josep said, smiling and chinking Daniel's bottle once again.

The beer went down smoothly. It was precisely what Daniel wanted, cold, sharp. Josep shouted out an order to a passing waiter, who returned with more beer. Daniel had a thirst on, it was clear. He found himself wanting to convey to Josep the strength of his feeling for Isla, how fortunate he was. Josep seemed to understand, both what he was saying and why he was saying it.

With the heat and the beer, things became distinctly heady as they tore at the little plates of food that were brought out in rapid succession, the waiter dropping the rattling dishes on the table as he rushed by carrying any number of other dishes for other tables: grilled prawns, aubergines, some kind of fried mashed potato.

Josep knew about the food, how it was prepared,

why it was good, what its origin was, and Daniel – two, three, then four beers down – was happy to hear him talk about it. His knowledge was impressive, as was the speed with which he spoke English, his fluency; it was as if, Daniel imagined, with just the two of them in freely flowing conversation, the language which Josep had learned all those years ago, when, as a young student in London, he had first known Isla, was properly coming back to him.

The dishes of food came and went. There were desserts: burnt custard, raspberries, an almond rice, all in little terracotta ramekins, each containing no more than three or four spoonfuls worth. Josep did all the ordering. Daniel didn't have to do anything, other than eat and drink. In the bathroom, he looked at himself in a cracked mirror. His face was flushed with the heat and his clothes were damp. When he returned, a fresh glass of beer was on the table. He looked at Josep and smiled.

'Last one,' he said.

'There's no rush,' Josep said. 'Let her rest.'

'I know. You're right,' Daniel said. 'But I can't help worrying.'

'It does you great credit,' Josep said, nodding and at the same moment raising his beer. 'To you and Isla.'

For the first time, it dawned on Daniel that Josep had been drinking as much as he had, and that he was similarly affected. 'Yes,' he said. 'To me and Isla. I'm sorry she's not here. She would have loved it.'

'I'm sorry, too. Although, if she was here, I suppose I would be somewhere else.'

'Where would that somewhere else be?'

'At Katya's.' He smiled.

'And who is this Katya?'

'Oh, a friend. More than a friend. I don't know. We have known each other for a long time and the situation remains the same.'

'And you'd like it to change?'

'Maybe. I don't know. I think so.' Josep leaned forward and drained the last of his beer. 'We go?' he said.

'Yes,' Daniel said. 'What about the bill?'

'There is no bill.'

'I can't allow it,' Daniel said. He was drunk.

'Okay,' Josep said. 'You leave the tip. However much you think.' He shrugged his shoulders and gestured to the table in front of them, covered in debris, prawn shells, bits of bread.

Daniel took out his wallet and counted out three ten euro bills and threw them onto the table. Josep gestured with his eyes to one of the passing waiters.

'You are a very generous man,' he said, patting him on the back as they stepped out onto the street. 'Too generous.'

As they sat in the car, waiting for the roof to come down, Daniel said: 'You're all right to drive, aren't you?'

'By the law, no, but by me, yes.' Josep smiled, released the handbrake and sped away from the kerb.

He drove quickly, weaving dextrously in and out of the traffic. On instinct, Daniel put his hand against the doorframe.

'Too fast?' Josep said.

'No, no. It's fine.' Daniel watched the city speed past, people waiting at crossings, hauling luggage down the street in the light of the sun. He looked at his watch.

'It's half past five,' he said, holding it up.

'I know,' Josep said. 'Isla will have had a good rest.'

Daniel thought of Isla, wondering whether he should text her and warn her of his return. He decided not to. They would, he reasoned, be there in no more than ten minutes. It was impossible to think of his life without her in it. This was the lesson of ten years of marriage: to be without her would be unbearable, like falling off a cliff and finding himself at the bottom looking up. He would be back soon, would be able to hold her in his arms, for the rest of the day and night if necessary; she wouldn't have to worry about Barcelona, or the things they had planned.

Josep pulled the car up to the kerb. Daniel thanked him and dashed into the apartment building. He couldn't wait for the lift and ran up the stairs, taking them two or three at a time. As he burst through the door, he was panting, hot.

'Darling,' he shouted. 'Isla!' but there was no reply. He passed through the bedroom on his way to the bathroom. The sheets were crumpled on the mattress but beyond that there was no sign of Isla. She would be out the front, perhaps asleep on the balcony, he thought, as he urinated, while at the same time calling out behind him: 'Isla! Darling! I'm back.'

When he finally went through to the front of the apartment, she wasn't there. The doors to both balconies hung open and a faint breeze was coming in. He went out onto the balcony, just to be sure. It was at this point that Daniel began, not to panic exactly, but to feel alert, as if his body or his gut were telling him that he needed to have his wits about him, that something was taking place that needed his attention. He went back through to the bedroom. Nothing. He went through to the second bedroom. Nothing. He went back to the first bedroom. He stood by the bed and called her phone. There was no answer. As it rang, he looked at her bags, which had been neatly placed against the back wall of the room. Alongside them, a small pile of clothes. It was the clothes she had been wearing earlier, neatly folded. It went to voice-mail. Daniel dialled the number again; still no answer.

All at once, he felt as if the ground had become unsteady beneath his feet, that it was in fact dis-appearing, crumbling and falling away and that he was tumbling through the air. But even as he felt that he was tumbling he felt also that he had seen this coming, almost precisely this, that he had, in fact, subconsciously predicted its coming, to him-self, as he and Isla had sat at the coffee shop having breakfast that morning, when Isla put the tele-phone down and told him of Josep's suggestion. He had known then – with a cold, iron certainty – that Isla would not be at the apartment when he returned. Despite this sense of having known what was going to happen, he still felt an equal sense of disbelief: this could not be happening; it was impossible.

He went back through to the other room. He

called her phone, again, and again it rang through to voicemail. He called the number Josep had left, no answer. Daniel went into a mania, tearing through Isla's belongings, her clothes, her bags, without a thought for what he would say on her return, desperately searching for some evidence of where she might have gone. He went into the bathroom. There was water dripping from the shower head, her toothbrush was wet.

Uselessly, he left the apartment and onto the streets, still trying to maintain an outward veneer of calm, thinking that she would have gone for a walk or a coffee. He went back to the café they had visited that morning, but she wasn't there. He walked on, not really knowing which way to turn, going into every coffee shop he passed, gazing through the windows of pharmacies and grocers. He looked up and down the pavement, wandering into the road between bursts of traffic to get a better perspective. For a moment, he thought he could see her, or her hair, bobbing between the heads of all the other pedestrians, but, in the end, he decided it wasn't her. The street was busy and hot, the air and movement oppressive. At each junction he seemed to catch the lights at the wrong moment and stood there, almost jogging on the spot, looking this way and that, waiting for them to change. He called her again and again, his thumb hovering over the redial button, but each time it went through to voicemail, and each time the thought that she might be on the phone to someone else receded.

When the street he was on came to a junction with a wide avenue, he sat down on a bench to gather his thoughts. He told himself that everything was fine, that he was overreacting. He phoned Josep, but there was nothing, not even a voicemail. He began to berate himself. He should never have gone for lunch. It was a disgrace to have left her, unforgivable. He would do anything to turn back the clock, to undo what he had done. When he resumed his search, he realised that he didn't know where he was, that he had taken so many turns that now even the direction of the apartment was beyond him. Everything around him seemed both familiar, that he had seen it before, and utterly new, that he had never seen it in his life. His vision started to feel a little strange, as if he were not looking through his eyes alone, but through a telescope turned the wrong way around. The whole thing was futile, a farce.

His phone rang. It was Josep.

'Isla's gone missing,' Daniel said. He could barely breathe.

'What, wait,' Josep said.

'She's not at the apartment. I'm out looking for her.'

'OK, OK,' he said. 'Calm down. I can explain.'

'What do you mean?'

'I mean I know where she's gone – or where she was planning to go.'

Josep explained: while they were in the restaurant, Isla had telephoned. She felt guilty about not feeling well on the trip and wanted to cook him – Daniel – a meal that evening. She had asked Josep for a good place to buy ingredients and he had suggested La Boqueria at the top of the Ramblas. 'If she walked,' Josep said, 'it will take her a while.'

'Oh Christ,' Daniel said. 'I don't believe it. I was frantic.'

'Relax,' Josep said. 'Go back to the apartment. Have a drink.'

Daniel did go back to the apartment. As soon as he got inside, he felt immense relief, as if the unthinkable had been averted. He went into the bedroom and rearranged Isla's things. His hands were still shaking and he didn't do it right, the piles were uneven, not as Isla had left them, but he would be able to explain.

He went back to the front of the apartment. The air was warm and the evening light came into the room. He stepped out onto the balcony and looked up and down the street. It was a regular Saturday evening in Barcelona. People sat at tables outside cafés. Isla would be back soon. They would cook together, eat, make love.

When he caught sight of her walking along the street, Daniel's heart leapt. He wasn't expecting her to be there at that moment. She was walking up from the cross street, carrying bags from the market. He could see a loaf of bread, a bottle of wine. He looked away and then looked back again, to make sure that his eyes were not deceiving him. It was definitely her. She was wonderful to behold. She moved hurriedly, her hair catching the light, her sunglasses back on her head.

At the pedestrian crossing she stopped and looked up. She saw Daniel and began to wave, a smile breaking across her face. She must have thought that he had not seen her, however, that he was frozen in some reverie, because she began to wave more vigorously, like someone from the deck of a ship. As she did so her arm must have knocked her sunglasses of her head. They fell forward and to the right. Isla's face changed into one of alarm as she stooped to grab them before they fell to the ground. In doing so, like an amateur juggler losing control of her batons, she succeeded only in throwing the sunglasses further forward and up into the air. Instinctively, she made a move to grab them, bringing her foot forward, but it caught against the bag she was carrying. It was going to cause her to stumble right out into the road, Daniel could see.

As Daniel watched all this unfold, the frames began to move more slowly. He had no conscious sense of what to do, but his mind – as if it wanted him neither to witness nor imagine what seemed about to happen – did something that he would not even remember. It went into a sort of delirium, as if spinning rapidly through a range of highly detailed landscapes, so detailed that Daniel could not possibly take them in, the succession of images overwhelming his cognitive processes until everything, including his awareness of where and who he had been, turned completely white.

He was on the patio of a bar, under an awning, having a drink with some friends. Somebody – it was Nando, he thought – was saying something, telling some anecdote. For some reason, Luis could not remember how the story had started and so he was finding it hard to follow, although everyone else appeared gripped. What was it about, he wondered. As he did so, his telephone rang. He answered it, standing up and turning away from the table. It was Penelope. She was excited, he could tell.

'Things are under way, Luis,' she said. 'My waters have broken.'

'They've broken?' he heard himself say. 'My god, are you all right?'

Of course, she was all right, she said. She was on her way to the hospital, her mother was taking her. Would he please hurry?

'Oh, my darling,' he said. 'I'll hurry all right.'

Luis leaned back into the table. He held up his hand. 'Nando,' he said. 'I'm sorry to interrupt your story, but I have to go.' He paused. He was as calm as he could manage, knowing the importance of the things that were about to transpire.

His friends looked up at him.

'It's happening,' he said, extinguishing his cigarette. 'She's in labour. I've got to go to the hospital.'

'It's happening! Fuck!' Nando said.

They all came forward at once, to touch his arm, to pat him on the back. They all knew that it was possible, but it wasn't expected to happen so soon. This was early, Luis knew.

'Can we help, Luis? Can we do anything?' Christina said.

'No, but I have to leave. This is it.' He could cry, right there, he thought; he wouldn't mind. He knocked back his beer and took his helmet from the table.

'Let me drive you to the hospital,' Roberto said, lighting one of his little cigars. 'My car's around the corner.'

'No it's fine,' he said. 'It will be quicker on the bike.'

'But you shouldn't drive,' Christina said. 'You won't be able to concentrate.'

'I'm fine,' he said. 'I have to go.'

They all stood and cheered him as he left. The bike was parked on the pavement. He straddled the machine and fired it up, testing the engine as he nosed it impatiently across the cobbles, people passing in front of him, unaware of the urgency, until eventually he dropped down onto the road, feeling the give of the shock absorbers.

He was away, out into the packed evening streets of Barcelona, that grand city where his heart had met its match. The sun slanted down through the trees. The machine throbbed beneath him, as if it knew that speed, its speed, was of the essence. He negotiated the cars, packed tight in the narrow side streets and then turned, with relief, onto Valencia, that wide, beloved avenue, with ample scope to overtake. He wove between the slower moving cars and buses, slanting his body, releasing the throttle, feeling the machine respond, the buildings flashing past as his speed increased. It wouldn't be long. All he could think of was the hospital and how to get there, what to do when he got there, whether he would have to wear a robe. He could see it all, could imagine it all: Christina lying back on a bed, him by her side, clutching her hand. As he rode through the streets, tears began to rim his eyes. It had been a question of choice, for both him and Penelope, a question of choosing the life that they wanted and leaving behind the ones that they didn't. And now it was happening. At the same time, it was the grandest of sacrifices, giving up one type of life, so that another might be born. He allowed himself to become carried away with it all and the tears flowed freely. At the hospital everything would change.

Up ahead, there were some lights. Out of habit – for all his bravado, he knew that really he was a careful man – Luis glanced at the pavement, to see what was what. To his right, he became aware of a woman walking quickly up one of the cross streets, looking up, not at the road, waving at something above. His fingers twitched against the brake lever. Suddenly, he wasn't sure why, her arms flailed in

9

1 x chicken +5

front of her and she stumbled out into the street, directly into his path. He was travelling fast, too fast. Christina was right. He couldn't believe it. He was going to hit her, this foolish woman, there wasn't time to react. Even as he thought it, however, as if some sixth sense, some instinct, were taking over, he found that he was easing back on the throttle, while putting every sinew into the action of shifting the bike's course. He didn't know how he was doing it, but he was. And then, like that – a flash, literally a flash – he missed her. It was by the narrowest of margins, but he was past her, fishtailing in an s-shape, until he recovered his balance and sped on towards the hospital, towards his wife, towards the woman who had transformed him.

Philip Langeskov was born in Copenhagen in 1976. His stories have been broadcast by the BBC and been published in *Bad Idea Magazine*, *Five Dials*, *The Warwick Review*, *Unthology* and *The Best British Short Stories 2011*. He lives in Norwich.

Extracts from 'The Overnight Bag' by Graham Greene are reproduced with kind permission.